Walt Disney's
MICKEY'S MILLENNIUM MYSTERY

by Ellen Weiss
illustrated by Gil DiCicco

MOUSE WORKS

Disney's Mickey's Millennium Mystery by Ellen Weiss
Find us at www.DisneyBooks.com for more Mouse Works fun!
Copyright © 1999 Disney Enterprises, Inc. All rights reserved.

For information address Mouse Works,
114 Fifth Avenue, New York, New York 10011-5690.
Printed in the U.S.A.
ISBN: 0-7364-1022-8

The Mickey Mouse Detective Agency was open for its very first day of business. Mickey sat at his desk, waiting for his first customer. He waited and waited, and then he waited some more. He was beginning to worry. Maybe nobody had any mysteries for him to solve!

All of a sudden, there was a rap at the door. It was his very first customer. He was a little unusual-looking, but Mickey didn't care. The visitor was going to hire Mickey!

"What can I do for you, Mister?" asked Mickey.

"Time," said the visitor. "Father Time is my name."

"Please have a seat," said Mickey.

"I have a big problem," said Father Time. "It's all about the millennium."

"Hmmm," said Mickey. "And what, exactly, is the millennium?"

"Well," said Father Time, "it's kind of like a very special birthday. We celebrate it at the beginning of the year **2000**. A year with a lot of zeros like that only comes once every thousand years!"

"Gosh," said Mickey. "That **is** special. So, tell me, what's your problem?"

"Well," said Father Time, "nobody can celebrate the New Year without me. That's why they call me Father Time, after all. And for the millennium, I need my very special millennium hourglass. I've been saving it for a thousand years, just for this moment, and now I can't find it! Here's a picture of what it looks like."

"That's a big problem!" Mickey said. "But don't worry, we'll find it."

Mickey was determined to do a good job of solving his first mystery. And it was an important one, too. If the sand in Father Time's special hourglass didn't run out, nobody would be able to celebrate the millennium. But how was he going to find the hourglass? There was nothing to do but start hunting.

The first place they went was Donald's house.

"Donald," said Mickey, "have you seen Father Time's missing hourglass? Here's a picture of it."

"No, I haven't," said Donald. "But I'm glad you came. I've been looking everywhere for my special party hats. I've been saving them to celebrate the millennium. I had four of them-one for me, and one each for Huey, Dewey, and Louie. I know they're here someplace."

"Let's see if we can all find them," said Mickey.

After they were done at Donald's, Mickey and Father Time went to see Minnie.
"Minnie," said Mickey, "have you seen Father Time's special millennium hourglass?"
"No, I haven't," said Minnie. "But maybe you can help me with a problem I'm having. I had a very special candle that I was saving, just to celebrate the millennium. It was in the shape of '**2000**.' And now I can't find it! Can you help me?"
"We can certainly try," said Mickey.

Next, Mickey took Father Time to Goofy's house.

"Goofy," said Mickey, "have you seen Father Time's special millennium hourglass?"

"Uh, nope," said Goofy. "But I was just looking for my lucky socks that I need to celebrate the millennium. I can't find them anywhere."

"We'll help you," said Mickey.

Mickey and Father Time kept walking down the street until they passed
Ms. Bingley's bookshop. Inside, Ms. Bingley was up on a ladder, looking
upset. They decided to go in.

"What seems to be the problem, Ms. Bingley?" Mickey asked.

"It's my millennium compendium!" she cried.

"Your—I beg your pardon?" said Mickey.

"My big millennium book. It has everything you could ever want to know about the millennium. And now it's gotten mixed in with the other books!"

"What does it look like?" asked Mickey.

"It's red," she said. "And it has the number '**2000**' written on it."

Next, they stopped by to see Daisy Duck. They found her in her garage.

"Hi, Daisy," said Mickey. "We're looking for Father Time's millennium hourglass. Have you seen it?"

"No," said Daisy. "And I haven't seen my millennium noisemakers either. I had six of them, and I can't find a single one. How am I going to celebrate the millennium without them?"

"Maybe we can help you find them," said Mickey.

They had still not found the hourglass. Where could Mickey look next? He decided to go see Uncle Scrooge. Maybe he would know.

But Scrooge did not know. He was too busy looking for his special **"Year 2000"** gold coin, and he was getting quite grumpy trying to find it among his other coins.

It was starting to get dark out. Nearby, Mickey spotted Pluto digging a big hole in the ground.

"What's the matter, boy?" Mickey asked.

"Oww-oww-wooww," cried Pluto.

"What's wrong?" asked Father Time.

"He's buried a very special bone," said Mickey. "I gave it to him for the millennium. Maybe we can help him find it."

It was getting late, and Mickey was beginning to run out of ideas. He was very disappointed. His first case, and he hadn't been able to crack it!

"Maybe we should just go back to my house," said Father Time. "Perhaps I put the hourglass away somewhere. You can help me look."

So off they went to Father Time's house.

As soon as they walked in, they smelled a wonderful aroma coming from the kitchen. "Yum!" said Mickey. "What's cooking?"

"It must be something Mother Time is whipping up," said Father Time.

In the kitchen, things were very busy, indeed. Mother Time was rushing this way and that, putting the final touches on the biggest cake Mickey had ever seen.

"Oh, there you are!" she said when she saw Father Time. "It's almost time for our party! Where did you go?"

"I went to look for my special millennium hourglass," said Father Time. "I've lost it, you see."

"No you haven't, silly," said Mother Time. "I borrowed it this afternoon, remember? I'm using it to make my Amazing 1,000-Year Frosting for my special millennium cake. It's been cooking for one thousand years, just for this big party. I even put a note on your sleeve to remind you that I borrowed it. Look, here it is."

"Oh, for goodness' sake!" said Father Time. "Look at that! Well, I'm very relieved. Now I can get ready for New Year's."

"Hmmm," said Mother Time. "Now, where is that hourglass, anyway? I know I put it down someplace."

"Don't worry. We'll find it," said Mickey.

At last it was time for the big millennium New Year's Eve party. Thank goodness Father Time had his hourglass, so everything could go the way it was supposed to.

Everybody was there! Even Huey, Dewey, and Louie got to stay up late. And when midnight approached, everybody counted down as they watched the sand run out of Father Time's millennium hourglass:

"Ten! Nine! Eight! Seven! Six! Five! Four! Three! Two! One! . . ."

Happy New Year!

Donald's hats

Minnie's candle

Goofy's socks

Ms. Bingley's book

Daisy's noisemakers

Uncle Scrooge's coin

Pluto's bone

Did **you** find all of the missing things for the Millennium Party?